gularabulu

Gularabulu
Stories from the West Kimberley

Gularabulu, 'the coast where the sun goes down', is an area of country on the north-west coast of Western Australia. These stories belong not just to Paddy Roe, but to all the Aboriginal people of this region. Whilst two of the stories are traditional myths, the others are of quite recent origin — since European settlement of the country.

With these stories Paddy Roe has attempted to communicate a picture of the life of his people. When he says that the book is for everybody, he is including white people, thinking that 'they might be able to see us better than before'.

The narratives have a gritty authenticity at which no other collection has ever aimed. The method of transcription helps the reader create the original oral form of the stories. The expressive repetitions, the rhythmic ebb and flow of the voices, the dramatisations, all give a rich sense of aesthetic qualities akin to poetry.

A challenge, a delight . . . no short sample could give an adequate sense of the vivacious, artful naturalness of Paddy Roe's recitations . . . a deeply beguiling book — Chris Wallace-Crabb, **Times Literary Supplement.**

A remarkable book . . . a new tradition in Australian Literature has just been born — Bob Hodge, **Westerly.**

Recommended to all who are interested in how Aboriginal identity came to be what it is, and as a sensitive evocation of Aboriginality as it was — Annette Schmidt, **Meanjin.**

Cover: *Mimia Spring* by Krim Benterrak. The painting represents a spring in Paddy Roe's home country.

gularabulu

Stories from the West Kimberley

Paddy Roe

edited by
Stephen Muecke

Fremantle Arts Centre Press

First published in 1983 by
FREMANTLE ARTS CENTRE PRESS
193 South Terrace (PO Box 320), South Fremantle
Western Australia, 6162.

Reprinted 1985.
This edition published 1993.

Consulting editor B. R. Coffey.
Designed by Susan-Eve Barrow Ellvey.
Cover painting by Krim Benterrak.

Typeset in 11/12 pt IBM Press Roman,
and printed by Lamb Printers, Perth,
Western Australia.

National Library of Australia
Cataloguing-in-publication data

Gularabulu: Stories from the West Kimberley

ISBN 1 86368 058 6
[1]. Aborigines, Australian — Western Australia —
Legends. I Roe, Paddy, 1912—, II Muecke, Stephen, 1951—.

398.2'049915

Contents

Introduction   i
Notes On The Transcription   x
Aboriginal English   xi
Pronunciation Guide   xii

The Stories
  Mirdinan   1
  Duegara   19
  Worawora Woman   29
  Yaam   35
  Donkey Devil *(Two Stories)*   45
  Lardi   57
  Living Ghost *(Three Stories)*   65
  Djaringgalong   75
  Langgur   83

Notes   93
Biographies   97

Acknowlegements

We would like to thank the University of Western Australia for financing the original Ph.D research from which this book emerges, and Susan Kaldor for supervising that research.

Frances Crawford and Kim Akerman first introduced us and were of continual assistance. The advice and comradeship of Nangan (Butcher Joe) and Dieter Kirchner provided constant encouragement.

We gratefully acknowledge the financial assistance of the South Australian College of Advanced Education in the production of the manuscript and the excellent typing of Margaret Weiss and Roslyn Leane. We would also like to thank Pru Black for proof-reading the manuscript.

Fremantle Arts Centre Press receives financial assistance from the Western Australian Arts Council, a statutory authority of the Western Australian Government.

Introduction

This is all public,
You know (it) *is for everybody:*
Children, women, anybody.
See, this is the thing they used to tell us:
Story, and we know.

Paddy Roe

The title of this book, *Gularabulu,* was chosen by Paddy Roe. It refers to an area of country along the coast of the West Kimberley of Western Australia. This coastline is characterised by sandy beaches, mangrove swamps, plentiful seafood and dramatic tides and currents. Gularabulu, "the coast where the sun goes down", stretches from La Grange in the south, through Broome, and north into Dampier Land as far as One Arm Point. As Aboriginal people from the various communities in this area meet regularly to engage in the activities of their culture, Paddy Roe stresses that these stories belong not just to him, but to all these people from the traditional tribal groupings of the Garadjeri, Nyigina, Yaour, Nyul-nyul and Djaber-djaber tribes. And when he says that the book is for everybody, he is also including white people, thinking that "they might be able to see us better than before".

Paddy Roe was born on Roebuck Plains Station, near Broome, just before the First World War. He was brought up there and learnt all the skills of working sheep and cattle stations. As a drover he travelled quite widely in the Kimberleys, then he was contracted for some years as a windmill repairer. These days he spends most of his time in Broome and on a small property in a locality to the north of Broome called Coconut Wells. A widower of many years, he is the patriarch of a large family, and in addition maintains a position of power as a kind of ombudsman negotiating between governmental agencies and the Aboriginal communities of Broome and its environs. By chance, initially, and later by hard work, he retains a good deal of knowledge of his traditional society.

Paddy Roe tells the story that his mother nearly killed him at birth because his skin-colour revealed white paternity. However his tribesman, Nangan, then a young boy, came to the rescue and took special care of him. If Paddy was to remain with his family, then the whites from Beagle Bay mission had to be avoided. In those days the practice of the missionaries was to collect part-Aboriginal children for education in the mission environment, a practice which effectively blocked their traditional Aboriginal education. On one occasion Paddy's mother hid him under a blanket as the people from the mission came looking for suitable subjects.

In consquence Paddy Roe grew up to become fully initiated as a member of the Nyigina. He retains not only a knowledge of the traditional stories, but also is a holder of a number of important ceremonies. Traditional initiation ceremonies take place in the West Kimberley every season and ceremonies and dance are transmitted from place to place. Paddy Roe plays an important part in the organization of this culture.

This book came to be made through research I was doing on story-telling in Aboriginal English in the Kimberleys. Most of the work was done with Paddy Roe, so I have selected some of the stories he told me.

There is a complex of factors which brought us together to do this work; these are the conditions which made the text possible. Apart from vague subjective factors like personal compatibility, there are other more general forces operating. One is the academic structure deriving from university departments. This structure sets up a line of difference, separating its culture (its economy, its organization, its concerns and beliefs) from that of another culture, which is always "the other". A kind of trade then occurs across this line of difference. Academics are sent out to "the field" armed with money and a knowledge structure which works to amass a specific kind of knowledge in specific ways. One of its techniques for the interpretation of other cultures is an attempt to " go beyond the surface of what is said in the field to work out the general principles underlying the culture".

Analysis is a necessary part of academic practice, but if it involves losing too much of the material that is important to the people being studied, then it should stop to examine its motives. It should assess the material produced, whether it be a book or an academic paper, to see if it is equally useful to the people who worked to produce it. It is for this reason that this book attempts to transcribe the stories, from tape recordings, as closely as possible. Other aspects of the book's organization obviously belong to Western culture: the way the story-telling event is represented in writing, the organization of the book as object (editing which unifies stories and gives them titles, notes, introductions), the modes of publishing and distribution which create a certain (largely non-Aboriginal) readership, and so on.

A related condition which makes the book possible could be said to be operating in the broader social arena, where work on Aboriginal "issues" (land-rights, medical and legal problems, new directions in training programs) continues to intensify and diversify. In this social environment there is room for more and more books to appear which in one way or another seem to respond to these changing theoretical and practical orientations. I hope that the conditions which have made this book possible continue to exist in ways which make more interesting and challenging work emerge from the Aboriginal—White encounter.

In relation to this particular volume, I would like to elaborate on some ideas concerning the types of stories, their transmission and social context. But first, I think I need to justify the way these texts are presented, and thus in part to criticize previous editions of Aboriginal stories.

Not all the stories presented here are recent; two are traditional myths. It might be argued that traditional myths or even more recent legends might be better presented as translations of the Aboriginal language in which they would have been told in the past. In that case, as with any translation, the reader would have to suffer the consequences of inexactitudes of translation where Aboriginal words, concepts, and linguistic structures did not match those of English.

Aboriginal English is a vital communicative link between Aboriginal speakers of different language backgrounds. It also links blacks and whites in Australia, so, as it is used in these stories, it could be said to represent the language of "bridging" between the vastly different European and Aboriginal cultures. It is therefore in this language that aspects of a new Aboriginality could be said to be emerging. The fact that it might be playing this important and interesting communicative role makes it seem purist and unnecessary to take traditional languages as a starting point.

There is another more circumstantial reason for presenting the stories in this form. Paddy Roe and I were in the habit of working with English as our means of communication, since I was not competent in any of the traditional languages which he speaks. When storytelling time came around it was still important for us that I should understand him and play the role of listener. The performance of the narratives depended in part on this listener response.

Of course, in my case, this listener response was of a special sort. As a white person, I represented for Paddy Roe a kind of generalized representative of white Australia. Accordingly I came to influence the texts to the extent that Paddy Roe addresses the "White Reader" at some points; he constructs scenes and characters in ways that show he is aware of European representations of scenes and characters. The texts are thus a message for a white audience, even if only at certain points. And as a listener I had a further role, that of transmitting this message.

The stories as they are presented here are word for word transcriptions from tape recordings. Hesitations and the occasional intervention from a listener are included. I have edited the texts to the extent of normalizing spellings (the few variations that do exist represent variations in Paddy Roe's pronunciation) and creating unitary texts by closing the transcription at what I consider to be the appropriate point. I believe that this is the first time that Aboriginal texts intended as narrative art have been presented in this way. Most editions of Aboriginal stories (originally told orally) have been written by Europeans. The translation from speech to writing, especially writing considered suitable for public consumption, involves editing which is massive in its proportions and implications.

Presenting the stories as narrative art is a way of justifying a writing which tries to imitate the spoken word. When language is read as poetic, it is the form of the language itself, as well as its underlying content, which is important. Just as it would be unjustifiable to rewrite a poet's work into "correct" English (in other words to take away the poets "licence"), so it would be unjustifiable to rewrite the words of Paddy Roe's stories. They are organized according to the conventions of oral narrative and can profitably be compared, at the level of narrative technique, with the stories of other cultures, such as Jugoslav epic songs and Polynesian oral traditions.

The simple act of writing down stories (as well as phrasing them in "good" English) inevitably involves departures from Aboriginal narrative style. To take one example, Hugh Edwards writes in his introduction to *Joe Nangan's Dreaming* (Melbourne: Nelson; 1976) about the difficulties he and Nangan had in communicating. The text resulting is loosely based on the content of Nangan's story, but its form and style is mostly Edwards':

> . . . *and still the eagle flew, her cruel shadow a black cross and a curse over the land below her soaring pinions.* *

This version does more than remove any linguistic or cultural difficulty which would have been present in Nangan's communication to Edwards; it *adds* the Christian symbol of the cross.

Because of attempts to make the texts in this collection true to the Aboriginal oral narrative style, the reader may experience some difficulty in reading the stories. Difficulty is a relative concept, depending on what the reader brings to the text in terms of knowledge. Some work on the part of the reader is therefore probably useful work, contributing to a better understanding of Aboriginal cultures.

---

* From the Djaringalong Story, p46. It can be compared to Paddy Roe's version in this volume.

Paddy Roe distinguishes between three types of story: *trustori* (true stories), *bugaregara* (stories from the dreaming) and *devil stori* (stories about devils, spirits, etc.). *Trustori* and *devil stori* are only produced as spoken narrative, while the *bugaregara* (the "law") may also refer to traditional songs, ceremonials and rituals of which there is a great variety.

Bugaregara stories are sometimes called myths; they are about supernatural beings who created land-marks, stars, rocks and rivers and gave mankind language and laws for conduct.

Trustori is the equivalent of our word "legend" — the characters of the story are human and can be located in time and space, within the memory of the narrator. The heroes of these stories can also perform fantastic acts.

Devil stori may be about quite recent events as well as distant ones. Here something inexplicable or anomalous happens which can only be explained by the presence of some spirit being. As Paddy Roe says, in connection with the alluring Worawora spirit woman:

> *Sometimes we see a woman pass but, when you look*
> *again you might say: 'Oh I've only seen a grass'. But*
> *it is the woman Worawora, she still lives today.*

What Europeans would call a perceptive illusion or hallucination is, for Paddy Roe's people, a glimpse "into" the world of spirits. Spirits can be seen all the time by *maban* (doctors), people who have enough "power" not to get disturbed by what they see.

Some stories from this region are about two *maban*; stories of this type may constitute a separate type. In them the *maban* or "clever men" protect their own people from evil.

Independently of the tripartite division of story-types which I have just made is another distinction, perhaps more important, between those stories which are *secret* and those which are *public*. Secret stories may only be told in the presence of initiated men of the tribe (this is in Paddy Roe's case; women have their own law from which he is excluded). In regard to the stories presented here, Paddy Roe made it clear in the epigraph that they are "all public". Five are *devil stori* – **Donkey Devil** (2) and **Living Ghost** (3) – **Djaringgalong** and **Langgur** are *bugaregara* and the rest are *trustori*.

These stories represent then, the continuation of an Aboriginal oral narrative tradition. It would be difficult to determine the point at which the stories were first told in English. Possibly some of them were never related in a traditional language.

The stories are definitely passed on from one person to another. Strict copyright sanctions exist for secret or sacred stories; the passing on of such narratives or songs must be announced publicly. These sanctions may be relaxed somewhat for "public" stories. Other people apart from myself were present at Paddy Roe's story-telling sessions. Even very young people were familiar with the stories and responded as active listeners when not inhibited by my presence. However, it is perhaps more likely that the narratives would be retained and retold by interested adults than by children.

The major social function of the stories lies in the way that they interact with and make coherent the present-day social context. Problems of law, alcohol, and European presence are presented in such a way that they are resolved in a dynamic of alternating reference between traditional values, physical aspects of the environment and the actual story-telling situation. But if story-telling is a way of solving social problems, in the sense of integrating and normalizing disruptive social events by absorbing them in narrative structures, this is not to say that the problems disappear entirely and forever.

The problems are still there, and though the ability to tell stories about them is some sort of comfort or therapy, this ability also has another power: that of transmission. Events cannot be transmitted in any raw state, they have to be normalized by some discourse such as narrative. The texts in this book are thus the means by which Paddy Roe has attempted to communicate a picture of the life of his people. He has attempted to give you pleasure in reading, a reading which is more like listening. In listening to him speak, you should listen for the techniques he uses to tell a story; nothing is deliberately hidden.

And in listening you should also try to hear what he is saying: that things have always been the same, but that they are different now; that as long as his people can speak out clearly, their culture will live on.

Stephen Muecke

Notes On The Transcription

The texts are divided into lines whenever the narrator pauses. The length of these pauses is indicated by one dash per second of pause. Hesitations in mid-line, at which points the breath is held at the glottis, are indicated by commas. Extended vowels, "growls" or breathy expressions are indicated by adding more letters to the extent of one per second. The texts are also broken up into episodes. The change from one episode to the next is indicated largely in changes of content: a change of character, place or time.

Aboriginal English

Some description of this variety of English should help readers be aware of linguistic features not present in standard English. Kimberley Aboriginal English often does not distinguish gender in pronouns (females are referred to as "he" or "him") and at the same time introduces *dual* pronouns which may explicitly include or exclude the person speaking or the person spoken to. Paddy Roe uses, though rarely in these texts, "yunmi" (you, and me) for himself and his addressee, "yuntupella" (you two fellas) for two people spoken to, excluding himself, and "mintupella" (me and two fellas) for himself and someone else excluding the addressee. Paddy Roe has partially adopted plurals for nouns, but alternates this with the Aboriginal English lack of plural marking on nouns.

Pronunciation Guide

Gularabulu, the title of the book, is pronounced with long 'u's', as in "food".

Aboriginal languages do not have the aspirate "h", so whenever Paddy Roe drops the "h" this is indicated in the usual manner (e.g. *'e* for *he*).

Where two consonants occur at the end of a word, Aboriginal English will tend to drop the last consonant (e.g: *mus'* for *must, kine* for *kind*).

Some features of the language as transcribed are typical of features of spoken varieties of English, such as the reduction of other final consonant clusters (e.g: *goin'* for *going*) and contractions such as *dunno* for *don't know*.

In Aboriginal storytelling, vowels are often extended or lengthened to indicate movement through space or time. In the text these extensions of vowel length are indicated by repeating the letter for the vowel (e.g: *riiight back to his country*).

mirdinan

A *maban* (doctor) is living with his wife. While he goes fishing she is having an affair with a Malay. The maban discovers them and later questions his wife who lies. On further questioning she admits to the affair and her husband kills her. He leaves camp and goes to join his countrymen, where the police pick him up to take him back to Broome. Halfway he escapes by magical disappearance.

The police pick him up again and put him in the lock-up in Broome. He again escapes by turning into a cat and being chased out of the cell by the sergeant. He returns to his people.

The police pick him up again and put him on the boat to Fremantle to be hanged. At the moment of hanging he changes into an eaglehawk and flies home. He makes a song on his return.

The police and people make him drunk to destroy his power, nail him in a box, and drown him in the ocean.

Woman as evil, lustful, unloyal, cause of protagonist's evil, act, + ∴ murder

MIRDINAN

Yeah ------
well these people bin camping in Fisherman Bend him
    and his missus you know --
Fisherman Bend in Broome, *karnun*[1] –
we call-im *karnun* ---
soo, the man used to go fishing all time --
get food for them, you know, food, lookin' for tucker --
an' his, his missus know some Malay bloke was in the
    creek, Broome Creek[2] –
boat used to lay up there[3] --
so this, his missus used to go there with this Malay
    bloke --
one Malay bloke, oh he's bin doin' this for --
over month –

so this old fella --
come back with fish one day he can't find his missus --
he waited there till late --
so he said "What happened to my missus? --
must be gone fishing ah that's all right" he said -
so he waited and he comeback he got nothing[4] --
"Where you bin?" he said, bloke said to him -
"Ah I jus' bin walkin' round" -
"Aah" -
soo all right next morning he start off again –
"Mus' be something wrong" this oldfella said --
oh he wasn't old but he was young --
said " 'e must be something wrong" -
so he went fishing --

*indicates
something
gone wrong*

3

he come back from fishing --
got all the fish comeback --
so he comeback on the other road --
near the creek, Broome Creek, you know –
comeback round that way --
when he comeback "Hello" he seen this man and
        woman in the mangroves, sitting down –
oh he come right alongside --
he seen everything what they doin' (Laughs) you know --
they sitting down --

so, he seen everything –
so he wen' back --
he wen' back home firs' --
he still waitin' for his missus -
his missus come up oooh --
prob'ly half an hour's time --
the woman must have give him time you know -
"Oh mus' be nearly time for my oldfella to comeback" -
but he was about half an hour late might be, his man was
        there already with the fish he was -
the oldfella was cooking --
fish, aaah they had a talk there --
that was about, dinner time --
now he said er --
"Where you bin?" -
"I wen' fishing –
err not fishing walkin' round --
I jus' lookin' round for shells you know" he said aaah –
ah –
"You can tell lie all right" he said --
"What for" he --
"Oh I seen you --
you and that Malay man" he said (Chuckle) "Yeah" -
"No no no no I dunno nothing about these Malay p -"
"Oh yes, I was there standing up right alongside" he said
"I know what's goin' on --
so never mind" he said "Tha's all right –

4

never worry" --
say "Come on yunmi better go^5 -- *you and me*
see if we can get some --
we go this way bush --"

they wen' bush --
oh 'long the beach you know very close to beach ---
"You bin goin' round with that Malay bloke tha's
    right?"
he tell-im --
that man --
"Yes" he tell-im --
aah --
he had tommyhawk in his belt --
aah --
well, yeah --
"You can see that one" he say ^{6} --
yeah that woman look -
he get the tommyhawk cut his neck right off -
with the to(haha)mmyhawk, finish --
head fall down -
then he start to chop him up then finish -
(Soft) in little pieces --
chuck 'em in the sea --
tha's the finish -

soo --
that fella wen' back -
to his camp -
pick up all his things what he had there --
pack up all his things -
an' he went straight to Thangoo Station --
Thangoo Station, there is a big camping ground there
    belongs to people too -
"Aah" --
"Aah" --
"Where you come from?" these people ask-im you
    know -

5

"I come from Broome" -
"Aah what about you missus where you missus?" -
"Oh I left-im in Broome" say -
"Oh, oh yeah --
what time you goin' to go back?" -
"Oh I go back in coupla days time" but coupla days
        time police already there (Laughs) -
lookin' for him --
police picked him up --
he had brother there too -
belongs to that woman, dead woman[7] -
"Tha's the man we gotta get" he said "tha's the bloke
        tha's him there sitting down" -
aah they come up police come up picked him up --
put a chain round his neck -
chain round his legs --
hand --
finish --

"All right" he say "We gotta take you back to Broome --
better come with us" -
"All right" he said "you bin kill your missus?" -
"Yes" he tell-im -
"Aha" --
now they took-im back -
they comeback ---
they camp in --
no they got early there --
they comeback for dinner -
half way -
the one governmen' well -
tha's Cockle Well --
Roebuck Plain --
so policeman and policeboy was very tired you know --
they dragged that bloke all the way -
like a dog you know with a chain[8] -- (Laugh)
walking -
footwalk -

and two bloke policeboy and policeman riding 'orse --
"All right we let the horses go -
let the horses have a –
rest (Exhales) you know -
let-im have a feed -
while we have our rest" -
so they let the horses go --
to take all the pack horses everything out packs --
they have their rest -
ooh till about -
three o'clock I think --
all right -
p'liceman tell his boy "You better get the horses I think
      now -
nearly time -"
all right -
policeboy go and get the horses -
bring all the horses back -
policeboy comeback -
policeman was packin' up all the gear -
plate an' billy-can an' everything puttin' them all in the
      pack you know ready -
tighten everything up ---
policeboy come straight up "Hey" he said "Where's that
      man?" -
policeboy sing out to police -
"He's under that tree" -
"Where?" -
they look round -
"Oh Chris' he's gone!" -
so they walked up there an' had a look -
the chain -
from his neck -
still got lock -
from his leg -
still got lock -- (laugh)
"Hullo" now they start thinking "What's wrong?" -
"Ooooh" the p'lice boy say "Might be tha's -

that man must be *maban* man[9] - doctor
he very clever man" -
"Yeah?" -
"Yeah" --

so they went back to Broome -
they couldn't find him -
no track -
where he come out -
his track where he was layin' down there -
but after that no track -
nothing -
so they came back -
Sergeant asked them blokes -
"Oh, you find the man?" -
"Yeah we found-im" – (Laugh)
"Where is he?" -
"Oh we lost him again –
here's the chain" -
they show that Sergeant (Laugh) –
"He come out of the chain jus' disappeared" --
(Gravel Voice)[10] "Aaaah doooon't" -
Sergeant never believe --
(Laugh) he couldn' believe --

so next time they went back again -
lookin' for 'im -
they hear that man is back again in the same place -
"Oooh he's back there" -
so somebody grab-im over there too --
that sister er brother belong to that sister -
you know dead, dead woman -
he grabbed (Laugh) that man -
and send somebody -
from there on foot right up to police -
"We got that man here we holding him" -
so police must come and pick-im-up -
they pick-im-up –

8

they went out for him pick-im-up again from same
     place -
he come with them right up to police station this time -
right up to police station --
right up -
right up to police station -
yeah -
"Here's the bloke -
tha's the murderer -
we got him now" -
"Oh good" -
"All right" he say -
Sergeant -
oh they got a few statement off him -
when they got the statement and everything off him
     they put-im in the lock-up, room -
oooh cemen' wall too -
old lock-up -
police station -
lock-up room -
lock-im-up --
put the key everything in -
all right --

soo --
ooooh bat --
five o'clock I think in the afternoon -
they want to give him supper -
Sergeant went there himself with the --
with the supper you know he bring supper for him -
tea -
go in there open the put the plates down and everything
     tea -
open the -
door -
he went inside --
have a look in the (Laugh) lockup room -
he's not there -

[handwritten margin notes: "repetitive devices", "almost as if he was there", "nar. is reliable", "drawing it out building up to big moment"]

he went all the place -
lockup you know, rooms -
nothing --
nothing -
couldn't find im -
"Aaah", *meow* -
meow -
one pussycat on top you know walkin' round -
(Growl)[10] "Aaah" Sergeant grab stick "Shh! go on! get
    out!" -
(Laugh) OUT he go through the door -
gone -
soon as he went other side er police station he's a man
    walking in the footpath (Laugh) -
he go 'cross the creek -
Broome Creek -
oh everybody seen 'im --
all the people seen 'im -

so police went round now look -
"We lost one bloke from --
from the police station -
you people seen-im?" -
"Yes!" they say -
"Where?" -
"He was walkin' along the footpath here -
he gone -
to Fisherman Bend same place again that way" -
but that was him -
he turn himself into cat - (Laugh)
an' Sergeant himself hunt him out from (Laugh) lock-up
    room (Laugh) -
so he went -
finish -
(Stephen: True Story?) Eh? (Stephen: True Story?) -
yeah, he gone -
finish -

sooo, when he wen' back they grab him again -
the same people --
same people -
oooh well he was thinkin' this time -
"I think no good" he say -
"My people don't like me" -
so they send one more man -
footwalk -
they grab that bloke they hold-im there --
a place called *kibilarid* --
that's where their camping ground is *kibilarid* -
that's in Thangoo country -
all right they come back --
policeman come again -
pick-im-up -
they bring-im right up to Broome --
this time they put 'im on the boat -
straight away -
boat was there too waiting -
they send him to Fremantle --
Fremantle --
they took him right up to Fremantle on -
the boat -
he was all right -
he was still in boat -
(Softer) he was on the boat -
he wanted to go too -
have a look at the country I s'pose (Laughs) he went
        right up to Fremantle --
they going to hang 'im --
hang 'im straight away -   *adresses*
'cos those days they hang people you know -   *and .*

all right they took-im right up -
must be hangin' place there too eh in Fremantle big
        place is it? (Stephen: Yeah) yeah well tha's right -
so they took-im there --
all right --

11

they gave-im last supper -
ooh feed anyway --
tucker you know -
after that they put-im on ah -
I dunno what -
mighta been some sorta flatform?[12] --
they put the rope round his neck --
they put-im on that one --
it's ready --
(Soft) straight away before he get out you know -
they had to do everything quick -
while he was there -
you know --
(Soft) all right --
(Breathy) they musta count --
from ten backward I s'pose (Laugh) you know --
they count -
he know too he, he know all that counting -
he was, he had the rope round his neck -
the LAST number --
the, that, flatform musta go down eh or something --
I, I dunno how they do that but (Stephen: Yeah, goes
        down) there's something, yeah -
right! GO! finish -
he fly out he's eaglehawk -
the loop was there (Laughter) the hang rope you know -
an' he's gone he's eaglehawk (Laugh) --
he fly away riiight back to his country (Laugh) -
(Stephen: Good one!) (Laugh) -
(Aside to Nangan) eaglehawk *iyena - ginyargu* -
(Nangan: Em[13]) -
waragan[14] you know, eaglehawk (Soft) he fly away --
(Softer) he was a eaglehawk then -

all right -
so when he land in his place -
he made a song -
for that one -

Fremantle -
you know --
he made a song now I gonna sing this song --
djabi, djabi song[15] --
I'll sing -
(Stephen: Mm) -

(Start high)
ah brimanta la la la wiriri
brimanta mudjaring ngalea
brimanta la la la wiriri
brimanta mudjaring ngalea
brimanta la la la wiriri (Growl)
brimanta mudjaring (Out of breath)
(Takes breath)
brimanta la la la wiriri
brimanta mudjaring ngale
tali minma walburu ridjanala
tali minma
tali minma walbur – *walburu ridjanala*
tali minma – *li minma walburu ridjanala*
tali minma
brimanta **la la la wiriri**
brimanta mudjaring ngalea
brimanta la la la wiriri brimanta mabu[16]

sooo that's im –
so I'll tell you what the meaning on that one -
(Stephen: Oh yeah, yes please) on the song (Stephen:
     Yeah) -
brimanta means Fremantle (Nangan: Fremantle,
     Stephen: Oh yeah) ---
(Laughs) you know but he never call-im proper, well
     that's Fremantle Fremantle *briiiimanta* -
la la la wiriri   'cos this man wanted to hang him had red
     clothes[17] –
(Stephen: Wiriri) *wiriri* -
wiriri means red -

you know (Stephen: *La la la* just tune) yeah *la la la*
     just tune *la la laaa wiririii* -
(Sings) *briiimantaaa la la laaa wiririii brimanta* you see
     he had red clothes -
that man wanted to hang this bloke (Laughs) --
and *mudjaring ngalea* -
mudjaring ngalea he bin run away *mudjari* -
mudjara means run away (Stephen: Yeah) -
run away -
mudjari -
mudjaraaa mudjariii ngalea that's his -
ngalea means that's his --
he had power in his -
in him you know -
in his belly[18] -
maban maban (Stephen: *Ngalea* belly) yeah –
(Sings) *mudjariii ngaleaaa* (Stephen: Why, why belly?)
     yeah -
an' *tali minma, walbaru ridjanala tali minma* that's
     telephone everybody bin ringin' up to hang this
     man (Laughs) (Stephen: *Minma*) on the telephone
     (Stephen: *Minma*, man?) eh? -
(Stephen: *Minma* is man) yeah – (Stephen: Is it?) -

   (Sings)
   tali minma walbaru ridjanala
   tali minma andjirili irbina
   njirili ibina njirili ibina

means the telephone -
njirili you know -
telephone -
poles -
(Stephen: Ya) that's, everybody bin ringin' up -
this man gotta get hanged today -
telephone -
taliii minma means he tell-im everybody you know -
just like he talk little bit in English too -

14

telephone you know (Stephen: Yeah *minma*) mm -

(Sings)
tali minmaa walburuu ridjanala
tali minma andjiliri irbina
tali minma walburu ridjanala

yeah --
they didn' know I -
they didn' know me he say I gonta fly -
gonta (Laughs) turn into eaglehawk -
that's when he kept that inside here -
in his, *maban* in his belly you know -
(Stephen: Mm) so that's all (Stephen: That's a beauty
that one) and that man name is[19] -
(Stephen: I got 'im – Mirdinan) ahh Mirdinan (Stephen:
Yeah Mirdinan) Mirdinan yeah -
huncle too -
my uncle I call-im uncle (Stephen: Oh!) (Nangan:
Mirdinan *ngadja*) *mirdinan ngadja* his name -
mirdinan ngadja -
this one[20] call him *djambardu*, grandfather (Nangan:
Mm *djambardu*) *djambardu* yeah grandfather -
call-im huncle -
(Stephen: That story's in your family!) (Laughs) yeah
yeah -
oh yes he's a family -
he belong to this country too (to Nangan) *ginja marda?*
he belong to this country (Nangan: Yeah yeah)
yeah he's our people -
seaside -
yeah -
he mix with (Nangan: Aaaall what **Njigina**) -
Nyigina Yaour Garadjeri everything he's -
we all one -
so he's one of our people too that fella -
you know this country people seaside --
ooh yeah[21] -

that's not the finish yet -
of the story --
that one (Stephen: Mm) -
but then people still -
when he come back -
now these people ask him -
"How did you come back? Where you come back
      from?" -
"I come back from Fremantle" say -
"Fremantle?" -
"Yes" -
"How you come back from Fremantle?" they said -
"I fly -
I bin turn meself into eaglehawk --
I fly from there right back to my country" (Laughs) -

and -
he come back from his country, that's from bush -
to these people where policeman used to pick him up all
      the time you know -
but these people didn' like him -
they still want the -
gibim to the police[22] -
if the police caan' do anything well they ought to kill
      that old fella too you know his own people -
(Stephen: Yeah) they ought to kill him -
same way like how this woman but they gave him -
they didn't want to get trouble -
from the police, they had to give-im back to police -

so they gave him back to police one more time -
and everybody gave him a drink, policeman gave him a
      drink -
made him drunk - (Laugh)
and they put-im on the boat and nail-im-up in the box -
you know they made a box for him nail him up inside -
chuck-im on the boat -
when they got halfway -

16

this bloke was drunk -
inside -
so he lost himself -
(Stephen: Mm) -
and they chuckled that -
they chuck-im overboard -
in the middle of the sea (Stephen: Oh) -
with the anchor -
or some sorta weight anyway (Stephen: Mm) -
so the box won't float -
so that's the finish of him (Stephen: Mm) -
he's dead -
that way -
they had to make-im drunk (Laughs) -
and the poor bloke -
they bin make-im drunk eh (Nangan: Yeah) -
yeah, an' he lose himself -
but he coulda come out of that box too if they didn' -
give-im drink -
(Nangan: Take-im outside Broome) -
yeah outside Broome, oh the middle of the sea -
(Nangan: That deep hole there) -
in er steamer passage you know -
in the middle of the sea -
but they put weight too so the box won't float -
so they got him that way -
but they had to give-im drink before they can (Laugh) -
before they can beat-im you know -
that's the only way they can beat-im, the some other
        ways they couldn' beat-im -
he was a very clever man -
this fella -
oh everybody know this story you know[23]

duegara

A young man steals a *maban's* wife. They elope. When they start travelling towards home again, they send an emmissary to inform the *maban* that he should come to fight for his wife in order to "make everything clear". The *maban* says "No, let them come here". They in turn refuse to come to his camp, so nothing eventuates.

At the place where the young man and the stolen wife are living, the men all go fishing one day while the women stay at home. A big storm blows up so the women shelter in a cave while the men hurry home. The stolen woman is sitting in the middle of the others. By the time the men get back they find that the stolen woman has been blown to pieces by lightning and all the others are unconscious.

The *maban* man had sent his power through the lightning and made it come up right underneath the woman.

woman as deceitful, lustful, unloyal
woman killed, not man

DUEGARA

bad man (phallas shaped stone)

"Yeah we'll talk about this *bugawamba* you know -
(Stephen: Yeah *bugawamba*) -
bugawamba that's that stone we show you[1] –

all right -
now -
this is old Duegara --
you know that's Duegara that's a true man you know -
he's a true person -
this time I seen 'im too -
old man he's a king -
Duegara -
he's a king --
he had his wife too -
married tribal way you know -
his wife -
so ---
this 'nother young fella come along he -
young man come along he pinch his woman -
you know take 'im away from 'im steal 'im -
run away with im -
took 'im 'way --
he took 'im riight up to -
Beagle Bay ---
Lombadina --
aall round that country he bin round there ooh nearly
        one year I think round that place –
and then he –
all these people come back now he thought this old fella

21

forget about this fella you know, well he had to
    come back to -
to make himself clear you know --
they must have a fight -
in tribal way --
to make it square whether he can give 'im this -
if they have a fight well he can let him have this
    woman --
if the old fella beat 'im well -
beat the young fella well old man will have to bring that
    woman back -
but if the young fella can beat him well he can take the
    woman -
it's that way -

so they all come back -
all the way from Beagle Bay -
they started from Beagle Bay they went back to Broome
    now on the beach you know all the way -
when they all come back -
he only went far as -
oh Barred Creek -
Quondong Barred Creek and Willie Creek -
Willie Creek -
now that Willie Creek you know I showed you that
    rock? that time -
that cave -
that's their camping ground if any rain -
but no rain they don't camp in the cave -
they camp outside --

all right -
somebody went into Broome -
from that place -
they told this old man -
"Well old man" they said "we bring this man back he's
    in Willie Creek now" they tell-im you know they
    tell old Duegara -

"Oh he come back?" -
"Yeah" -
"Woman and man come back" -
"Yeah" -
"And what he say?" -
"Well we come up to pick you up -
bring you back to Willie Creek to pick up your missus -
you know your woman" —
"Oh good --
well" he say "I won't go --
they can stop there -
in Willie Creek, I'm not going -
I don't want to pick 'im up -
if he want to come back there well let 'im come right
      back here but if he don't want to come back well
      let 'im stop there I won't go" –
"Oh", so this man went back he tell these fellas -
"Oh we bin want to bring old man so you can clear -
make everything clear you know fight out here -
but the old man won't come" -
"Oh" -
"So I think you better go" -
"No I won't go" say --
this man and woman said "No we won't go -
let 'im come here" -
"Ah" -
so this man went back again -
ah -
back to Broome -
he tell 'im "No they not goin' to come" -
"Oh well leave them -
I don't want 'im" say -
"I don't want the woman" he say
"Let 'im have 'im -
he can have the woman" -
"Oh good" -
so this fella come back again -
he tell these fellas -

23

"All right that old man said no more he -
he don't want any trouble -
no fight no nothing -
so you keep the woman" -
"Aah all right" he say –
but this man know too - ⁊

so one day -
they went out in the cloudy day too but it's rain time
        you know this is the rain time –
that's why I show you that -) MF
cave you know where that's their place where they -
go in -
from rain you know -
(Stephen: *Yubyub*) -
no rain time this is different *manggala*² -
manggala manggala rain time -
dis is *manggala* -

all right –
four there was about -
five man -
five man and five woman -
they, camping in that ground -
so these five man went looking for fish -
they go through the creek -
come out other side -
they went other side gettin' fish -
oh long way you know you seen that creek -
where he run they went that way -
and these womans all sit down home -
in that little island now -
langunguru we call 'im – (Stephen: Mm mm)
(Soft, breathy voice) they siddown -
all riight -
oh big rain you know cloud coming up -
biig cloud -
biig cloud -

24

soon as he come close you know ooh lightnings
    everywhere -
biig lightning -
strike everywhere -
"Oh we better rush back" these fellas said -
big rain comin' they had lotta fish too -
they all run back this five man -
and five woman there too –

all right when these womans seen all these, whatname
    comin' you know the rain -
oh they pick up all their -
blankets and tucker whatever they had you know put
    'im aall inside -
and the cave is like that – (Draws)
you know that's where they go in from -
the cave is more like that you know -
that's the place they go in -
this is their door -
to go in -
and this is all rock you know on top --
that's the island like --
that's the island runs right around you know every-
    where --
that's their place camping ground --
proper too from *bugaregara* you know[3] -
long time -
well that's their camping ground in that island (Fade) -

(High) all right -
oh the rain start now straight away -
so they all went in -
that woman was here in the middle they put 'im -
he got four womans here -
see four woman oh they got dogs too -
they had some dogs inside -
four woman -
there's one woman -

'nother woman 'nother woman 'nother woman and here
    him in the middle --
they put 'im in the middle --
ooh they know lightning everywhere --
biig lightning, everywhere strike -
these man comin' ooh still long way from creek —
very hard —
they come they had big load too fish -
so this lightning now -
rain rain rain rain rain jus' pouring -
now ONE LIGHTNING COME -
he strike -
he strike right underneath this woman -
you know ah -
lift 'im up -
chuck 'im outside -
pieces and guts head -
oh liver heart everything -
aall pieces everywhere -
and this woman was in the middle -
this two --
four woman here you see they put 'im in the middle -
but the lightning come from right underneath him -
lift 'im up just chuck 'im through the door in pieces and
    finish -
and aall this other four woman -
two fall down here inside you know - (Laughs)
and 'nother two here too they only laydown just
    outside here -
only one woman he lift him out from the -
from that cave chuck 'im right out pieces -
dogs (Laugh) -
all layin' down --

(Soft) all the man come -
(Soft growl) hellooo "Hello might be something wrong"
    that man said -
that lightning strike right there -

they couldn't see too -
lightning you know -

so they all come up they look -
hello they see two woman layin' down outside and
  'nother one is all pieces --
hello which one -
they look round 'nother two woman layin' down here
  inside -
'nother two here -
and this fella he just -
he lift 'im from there chuck him outside pieces - (Laugh)
aall in little pieces -
leg hand head liver everything (Laugh) pieces --
"Mm-mm" --
dogs all big sleep -
all come up there look oh they start to cry now -
they know straight away -
"Oh my woman bin get killed" -
"Yeah" -
"My woman get killed" -
"Yeah" --
all cry now all them man, ah these fellas don't know --
they crying crying crying crying -
one woman get up --
one woman -
"What's wrong?" he say -
"What yupella crying for?" -
"Oh lightning bin hit you fellas -
yeah" -
"Oh -
yes?" -
"Yes" -
"And what yupella crying for?" --
"One woman -
finish" --
he look -
aah (Laugh) pieces -

'nother woman get up again, 'nother one inside -
they all get up one by one you know –
all get up finish --
they come out right dogs all get up too (Laughs) -
all the dogs not one dog got killed -
or them other four woman nothing -
only from shock I s'pose eh (Stephen: Mm) --
the lightning -
(Stephen: Yeah) -
yeah jus' fall down -
but only one he only wanted one woman -
couldn't get 'im from any other way so the lightning
        come out from underneath -
to lift 'im out -- (Laugh)
now this is the magic belongs to black man - (Laugh)
(Stephen: That's Duegara) that's Duegara -
(Stephen: That's Duegara who did that) mm –
that's why he said to this man we don't, I don't want
        that woman he can stop there that man can have
        'im -
but he know he wouldn't have 'im too long –

that's his thing there now that *bugawamba* –
(Stephen: That's the same man) -
same man, he went in his dream -
he make that fella into lightning -
kill that woman (Laugh) -
that's him -
that fella now -
that's him that's his spirit --
sometime when we go past "Hello" -
don't go there that's old man there they say you know,
        (Laugh) womans -
we know Duegara --
so we only bin show you stone you know -
soo --
that's how powerful that thing is

Moral seems to be that black man's magic is
powerful enough that anyone who commits a
crime against trad. Rules will inevitably pay
for it.

worawora woman

is soc.
polygamous?

A fine strong man used to provide handsomely for his two wives by hunting.

One day he thought he'd see if the *worawora* woman really existed, so he painted himself up in the required way. He left his camp and went to the right tree where the woman came out to meet him.

They hunted together, but when he wanted to share the hunt between her and his women in camp she refused, taking all the food for herself.

The man went back home empty-handed. His wives questioned him, he said he could find nothing.

Everyday he went to this woman and the same thing happened. Eventually he revealed the truth at his wives' insistence.

Then he went and decapitated the woman.

WORAWORA WOMAN

Well this man proper man had two woman in camp[1] --
an' he's a strong man that fella well I mean he can feed
    that two woman -
that's why he's strong you know he, he can get lotta
    food -
walkin' you know --

well he used to kill (goanna) -
everything -*emphasis*
bring pl<u>ee</u>enty o' meat you know plenty everything
    tucker for these two woman --

so one day come ---
that old fella paint himself with everything -
he want to find this woman if it's true[2] --
it's true all right he come out in 'im -
so he got this woman too an' he got nother two over
    there proper womans in his camp you know --
all right -
oh this woman foller 'im round he got his, thing too, to
    carry --
everything what that man kill you know[3] (Stephen:
    Yeah) -
tucker for them two women too --
all right -
oh he got 'nuf dis -
coolamon is full now you know with the tucker goanna
    everything -
"Oh well that 'nuf" -

strong man = good hunter ∴
    + women
31

all right he -
he stop in one, tree -
they siddown -
"All right you take this one" -
he tell that woman -
"An' I'll take this one back to my 'nother two woman
        in camp" -
"No" he say --
"No you not takin' anything back it's all mine" --

(Laughs) he come back -
come back in his two woman --
so that woman disappeared with his tucker an'
        everything it's gone --
this man goback oh he's too tired now can't get
        nomore -
everything enough to goback home he's hungry ---
he had two woman waiting for im --
see --

coming back w/ nothing indicates something wrong

only with spear hunting stick tommyhawk in his belt --
"Ooh what wrong?" they tell-im -
"No no got nothing" he say "I been everywhere can't
        find anything" --
he didn' want to tell, these two woman -

ah --
he's bin doin' this for aaaall the time -
so this man off dis way -
but that woman is there too -
he kill eeeverything what he can get he pull everything
        out of his belt -
that man you know put-im in his little, that thing -
he must carry all them things -
he bin doin' this for ooh -----

(Speaks to Butcher Joe in Nyigina)
smoke -
all right?[4] -

32

no I means -
he just asked me if -
that smoke all right, eh -
it's not -- (Stephen: Oh that's all right) aah (Stephen: He
        wants to move?) no he's all right too –

aah so one day come -
"Ah well you bin little bit too long comin' back with
        these things" he tell-im "No tucker" -
these two woman tell-im --
"You must be got somebody" –
tell-im, you know these two woman say --
"Might be some woman somewhere" –
oh they know too the womans know too –
"Aah yes" he tell-im "Yeah -
that's that woman" -
aah all right "Well we gettin' hungry look at all the kids
        all gettin' hungry no tucker --
you only feeding one woman" -
"Yeah tha's right" he say "Tha's true" -

so he went back again he kill everything --
finish all right -
they siddown under the tree now, that -
aall that goanna what dis man got he puttin-im in the
        same dish again you know that thing -
this man off one side 'e get that tommyhawk from his
        belt an' he cut his neck right off -
finish (Laughs) (Stephen: Oh) kill-im, dead -
finish -
'e didn't want to kill-im but 'e had to do it -
other way they all die from hungry too -
the people -
so he kill that woman -

but that's only one -
it's lots more, yet -
(Laughs) you know (Stephen: Mm) -

33

he only done this jus' to try -
this person, you know -
he done this jus' to try -
but we all know too -
there is a woman there -

but we gotta be painted up with the different trees -
you know -
gotta be painted up with different trees -
we bite all the leaves and skin you know off the trees
        an' we gotta paint –
sit down under that tree then the woman come
        (Laughs) -
I know it's very hard for somebody to believe, you
        know (Stephen: Mm) It, it's dere -
it's there -
(Stephen: Aw, sounds all right) -
(Laughs) yeah –
yeah -
Oh some, lotta people done these things too, you know -
lotta people done paint themselves

yaam

Yaam is a marginal character, a madman who imagines that the cattle he lives with are his lost countrymen. Paddy Roe describes an old custom of self-punishment when re-entering camp, and how Yaam couldn't ever accept clothes or food. He finally died when a tree fell on him during a cyclone.

YAAM

Yaam --
(Rasping starts)[1]
used to camp on his own --
aaall the time ---
he walk around naked too (Rasping stops . . . tap tap) -
walk around naked --
oh not very long this one I was -- (Rasping starts)
I musta bin big boy too I think ---
fifteen sixteen might be seventeen --- (Rasping stops)
I know (Tap tap) these people used to come through
        with the cattle too from Beagle Bay you know --
they used to bring bullock for boat shipping, ship
        (Rasping) --
for steamer -------- (Rasping stops)
and er --
when the wild cattle come in for drink -
to that spring -
wonganad spring -
he come with them too --
that fella --
he come with the cattle --
oh cattle know im (Laugh) -
wild cattle -
but (Rasping) when they see two people -
mule and horses and people you know these bullock -
they run away -- (Rasping stops)
very wild -
wild cattle all scrubbers -
scrub cattle so he used to mix up with these bullocks

too this old fella ----
he used to mix up with these bullocks –
so he walk along the road you knooow –
one day they comin' up -
these fellas were camping there Beagle Bay he had
    Brother[2] there too I dunno which Brother --
one of the Brothers anyway -
stockman you know Brother --
"Oh Brother" they said "er this man might come out in
    us --
might be soon (Tap tap) -
might be tonight or might be this afternoon" -
"Oh yes" he say (**Rasping**) "**Some**body round here?" -
"Yes --
we call-im *Yaam*, he's a cranky man[3] --
he's a proper Carnot Bay country –
Djaberdjaber people" –
"Ahh good -
ah well if he come we'll give-im some tucker" - (Rasping
    stops)
Brother said you know (Tap tap) "Ah yeah –
I dunno" --
say -
"Yeah we can give him tucker -
I dunno whether he'll eat tucker -
but we'll give-im -- (Rasping)
he can't eat tucker too he don't know" – (Rasping
    stops)

so they all waited there -
one afternoon all right they can see some dust coming -
in the cattle pad you know they look "Oh bullock
    coming" (Breathy) shh all stop quiet -
you know people in the camp -
here these bullocks coming longside --
coming closer and closer --
when they smell you know bullock --
(Sniffs) they goin' like this you know -

they can smell somebody's there in the water (Laugh) -
in the waterhole --
horses and people too you know smell -
(Breathy) an' this man stand up they look "Oh there,
    there that man! there that man in the middle right
    in the middle of the bullocks" -
in the cattle pad too they all walking same road -
he stand up too watching just like these bulls you know -
watching and he go like bull you know he go too (Sniff)
    (Laugh) same thing madman you know -
aaah finish - (Rasping)

all right –
they come right up - (Rasping stops . . . tap tap)
oooh they come up little bit more close all the bulls run
    away --
oh these people they only leave that man standing up –
he off too behind (Laugh) -
same -
he follow all his mates you know bullocks -
wild cattle -
come back -
"Ah now he come back again" from halfway --
he leave all the bulls all them cattle standing up -
watching this side -
he walk back --
he got his tommyhawk in belt -
he bin runaway with that tommyhawk long long time
    ago -
he got his tommyhawk -
he got his *naul*[4] -
he got one *karli* two, two *karli* -
two *karli* and dis one *karpina* shield you know -
karpina -
he come right up -
all right he come out in these people -
all these people all sitting down you know -
(Soft) aaall sitting down -

waiting for him he comin' up all the pack horses and
    mules you know all pack mules an' riding mule all
    feeding -
he stop put all his *karlis* down an' everything then he
    come out for these whatname, mules you know -
(Creaky voice) "C'mon youfella wanta throw-im *karli*
    for me[5] (Laughs) -
I bin lose all our people" -
I dunno what people but you know -
he come out in this lot oh good way too very good way
    that's the way the old people do he musta still have
    that in his head you know only that one thing –
"pppppppp" you know what kind these mules go
    "ppppppppp" -
"Ah ooh" they go (Knocking on forehead) (Laughs) hit
    themselves with *karli* "eeeeeeeee, eeeeeeeee" cry
    you (Laugh) know for dead people -
mm all right from there they tell Brother now "Brother
    he gonna come up to us now" -
we wait for him --
all right he come up alongside -
he put all his things down again -
come out with only one *karli* and one shield --
"C'mon youfella throw-im *karli* for me I bin lose all
    our people" -
I dunno what people - (Laugh)
"Nooo he all right" they tell-im -
'nother lot old old fellas get up you know they tell-im
    "Nooo don't worry about, that nothing you come
    up here -
right up to mepellas -
we can't growl you for that things you know -
can't help you bin lose all our people, mm" oh he
    come up "weeeeeeeeeeeeee" you know he hit
    himself with *karli* for these people Brother too
    whole lot (Laugh) -
whole lot finish --
all cry -

'nother lot liar you know jus' make-im fool this fella[6]
    "Uuuuuuuuuuuuuu" everybody Brother and all I
    s'pose (Laugh) -
yeah he get happy now --
oh they give-im tobacco meat bread everything, clothes -
Brother give-im trousers and shirt straight away -
he had no clothes naked he walkin' round -
no clothes nothing mm ---

all right -
"Well you better camp here with us -
only one night you know we must keep you here" --
"Yeah all right" he say --
all right -
he stop with these people little while - (Rasping starts)
they talk-talk all talk language ---
all talking language --
after talk-talk (Rasping stops) ---
(Rasping starts) ooh might be just about eight or nine
    o'clock I think you know, they talk right up to
    about that time (Rasping stops) nearly sleep time -
"Well" he tell-em "I gotta go now" ---
"I bin leave some people behind I gotta (Laugh)
    bring-em back all this tucker an' everything for
    that lot -
they must be waiting for me -
you know they get hungry" he say -
"Oh all right then (Tap tap) how many people there?" -
"Oh too many" he tell-em --
must be all them wild bullocks you know cattle -
he go back -
oh he only go back from here to that, tree there I think -
that little leaf hill there see -
that far -
he stand up there put his tucker down everything he just
    take his clothes everything out shirt everything just
    leave-im there (Laugh) eeverything -
mm flour -

flour you know tucker just leave the lot whole lot
    everything there tea sugar -
he jus' take his gear that's all finish gone --
used to do that aaall the time you know (Rasping
    starts) -

(High pitch) oh not very long ----
this is round about --
nineteen twenty-seven --
must be round about nineteen twenty-seven - (Rasping
    stops)
twenty-seven twenty-eight twenty-nine thirty -
twenty-seven twenty-eight you know -
dis one -
I was (Tap tap, rasping) oh --
all ready big boy --
ah that's the last they seen 'im --
oh they didn't want to take 'im home or anything they
    know because he's only mad man (Stops rasping) -
if they take 'im back he'll still go way you know they
    didn't want to take-im away from the country -
so, yeah I was big boy all right --
that time --

so one day big cyclone come --
biig cyclone --
aall over this country you know --
big cyclone come --
when that big cyclone came -
rain rain rain daays and daays -
biig cyclone too, wind -
big rain was first then cyclone came after -
(High pitch) so he made his camp under the tree -
big, paperbark tree oh big tree about that big you know -
little bit laying down -
like dis you know -
like dis one'ere -
he made his camp underneath, there --

(High pitch) and that tree fall on top of him that's the
    thing killed him (Stephen: Mm) in *wonganad* -
that old fella he got killed in the tree -
with tree, tree fall down on top of him he couldn't get
    out -
he died finish --

(High pitch) and when I come to this station –
from Roebuck Plains you know I was man then
    already --
to the station and we used to go mustering around
    wonganad -
(High pitch) they show me the tree –
you know the tree fall down -
and his bone -
bone but his bone was very, like ashes you know
    (Fingers leaves) **very** soft -
this way he die -
we only dig -
dig you know dis kind (Digs) –
the bones -
we cover-em up again -
we talk too, we talk to 'im --
"We only jus' come up to visit you know" we tell 'im -
so, "We put you back again inside" -
this is your home" –
so he never trouble us no more (Laugh) you know --
well I seen his bone too -
he was a true man (Rasping starts) -
he not *rai*[7] but he mad man -----
and why they didn't —
well because those days nobody never worry about
    people --
you know anybody --
whether to make 'im good ooor let 'im go bush let 'im
    die in the bush you know that's what they used to
    do to them --
so --

different this time -- (Rasping stops)
that's why this old fella lost his life (Rasping starts) --
I s'pose --
in his way too how he wanted to, live -- (Stephen: Yeah)
you know (Stephen: Yeah) (Tap tap, rasping) -
I dunno what made 'im mad in the first place ------
they never tell me how he get mad --
might be from that same place in *wonganad* er
     wardubarany I dunno --
he come from up that part of the country too (Rasping
     stops) ---
old *Yaam* (Rasping starts) ----------(Tap tap tap)

donkey devil

Story One

During the war Paddy Roe got drunk one night. On his way home he didn't see anything, but two men following him were frightened by a strange animal with donkey ears and a big bushy tail. They took Paddy back in the morning, but they couldn't find any tracks.

Story Two

One day Paddy went to work while his wife and her friends went fishing. In the afternoon his wife came running back because they had been frightened by a devil. At a forked road they had seen a strange animal with donkey ears and nose and tail like a dog. They had dropped all their things and ran.

So Paddy took his weapons and went to investigate. When they got there they could only find the women's tracks and no sign of the devil.

DONKEY DEVIL

Story One

Well war time you know I used to (Rasping) —
war time I used to drink ---
so I got drunk -
one day you know we all had drink -
war time -
we never worry you know er -- (Tap tap)
we don't want to be frightened then[1] - (Rasping)
we don't think about nothing –
I only bin drink for reason too you know ----

so -----
one day I come back late --
oh not too late but early - (Tap tap, rasping)
might be --
eleven o'clock or something like that -
I went back home I went past that -
old place there you know (Rasping stops) shire council -
institute --
institute --
shire council – (Rasping starts)
oh road board –
road board office ---
we used to call-im ------ (Rasping stops)

now when I went past I never see anything ---
I never see nothing --
so 'nother two bloke was comin' behind me -

Brumby and Phillip (Rasping starts) oh they drunk too –
they had too much drink too —---
so when they come up very close —
nobody close to that place —
one big gum tree there (Rasping stops) -
where we always pull up in the bank –
here -
Commonwealth Bank -
that big tree –
yeaaah -
they look -
they hear the noise you know -
like boots (Bang bang) goin' like this (Bang bang bang,
      beating ground) -
yeaaah -
they look -
oh (Soft) something standing up -
they look -
donkey -
donkey -
(Soft) when they see donkey –
(Deep voice) he got his ears -
earhole you know like this – (Laughs)
"Ah that's the donkey" they say "Yeah, where he come
      from? somebody musta lost donkey here
      somewhere" –
"Yeah must be oh we better leave-im" they say -
tupella off -
soon as tupella off from here to this, pole here he go
      like this again (bang bang bang) -
they look back -
he come out more in the open now dis -
"Oh he's a donkey" they say -
"Yeah" ah -
he goin' this way now -
you know he shake his head –
blugblblbup (Laughs) his earhole -
when they hear that one (Clap) that two bloke off

(Laughs) --
they stop (Soft voice) -
near the church -
they look back -
they look -
"Oh he's here behind" -
standing up again -
they look (Soft) "Oh he's donkey" –
"Must be donkey" -
"Yes donkey" -
"Oh we better leave-im" -
he shake his head again like this you know
       blubububurub (Laughs, clap, clap, clap) -
off! (Clap) that two bloke -
when they bin come right up to Matso's store you know
       that, store (Stephen: Yeah) -
they stand up again -
they look back again oh he's still here -
yeah --
he shake his head again hohoooo! -
an' they look proper -
there's donkey earhole –
and tail is like a dog -
woolly -
you know woolly tail -
oh when they see no no no this must be devil - (Laugh)
(Clap) last –
one bloke in the lead -
'nother one behind –
they put last speed on (Laughs) they can't go no more -
they come out in – (Pant pant pant)
what's wrong I say --
"Arrrgh (Growl) devil we bin see-im donkey -
devil" -
"Yeah?, arrgh go on" I say (Laugh) -
I was 'sleep -
I never take any notice -
I don' want these fellas to make noise -

so dey -
next mornin' they tell me -
"We show you dis track" dey tell me -
"All right" I say -
we walk riiight up to that place nothing only two man
     track running -
no donkey nothing -
no nothing –
now where they first see this donkey in the, (Rasping
     starts) under that tree --
that's the place they bring me -
right up to that one -
but noo track nothing (Laugh) –
soft ground --- (Rasping stops)
so that's er --
that's about (Rasping starts) –
tha's that one (Rasping)

Story Two

Yeah well from there --
oh three week --
might be -
three five or six weeks time you know I –
I finished there then in Governor Broome -
in that ice works -
they shift me back to Roebuck -
this time --
Roebuck Hotel –
they bring me back there --
tha's same -
same boss -
but he had two factory -
ice -
(Rasping starts) icework you know –
lemonade ice -
I used to do the same job in 'nother place too ----

so I shift all my camp and everything I bought meself
        little house in ---
Morgan's Camp you know *burgugun* -
we call that place *burgugun* -
so I bought a little house for meself --
oh about fifteen pound - (Laughs, starts rasping)
fifteen pound one good little house --
jus' 'nuf for me an' my old woman an' my children –
two, three children ----- (Stops rasping)

so one day come --
these old fellas wanted to go while -
me and old woman was having supper –
my old woman he said to me -
"Oh tomorrow I think me, this other two old woman
        we gotta go fishing -
think all right?" -
"Yes!" I tell-im, "You fella can go get some fish (Tap

tap tap) for down the creek" -
"Yeah we gonta go" -
so they had they --
my old woman get his line an' everything you know
    put-im in the bag -
hook sinker everything –

(Rasping starts)
so these fellas off now --
next mornin' -
they off -
all right I went to work -
jus' pull ice out -
I went very early --
four o'clock in the morning I start pullin' out ice -
    (Laughs) (Rasping stops)
pulling out ice four o'clock in the morning --
cut all ice an' everything up –
put-im in the cart –
horse an' cart - (Rasping starts)
I sell all the ice round -
an' these three woman they off ----
'bout six o'clock ----
they're off, to creek -
fishing (Rasping stops) when they went there --
they went right up there ---

all right -
there's two road there you know er -
one road they come this way 'nother road turn this way
    to creek nother one this way -
like a fork you know -
that road ah -
they look -
in that road ---
they look --
oh donkey layin' down -
(Laugh) you know -

donkey -
ah not donkey but -
(Young Girl: Dog)[2] er dog dog -
he got his earhole like a donkey too -
but when he look this way he's a dog (Laugh) you
     know -
he's a dog –
yeah -
an' he's watchin' these fellas -
when they look proper -
his tail goin' this kind you know he moving -
his tail woolly tail -
donkey earhole and nose like a dog --
(Young Girl: Dog) -
oh when they seen that that's all they only seen that tail
     moving -
oooh! them three old woman (Clap) OFF (Laugh) they
     lose all their fishin' line an' everything -
bags all behind -
water with billy-can (Laugh) jus' chuck-em -
off they went –
that was all wet ground too from tide you know –
oh these three woman fall down everywhere slippery
     very slippery you know -
so they only jus' trot along slowly 'till they got there -
but I was there all ready -
you know in home -
old woman come "Hey" -
(Breathy) "You got any fish?" -
'NO no no no" he tell me -
"What wrong" -
"Devil we seen-im there" (Laughs) "Big dog or
     donkey" -
"Yeah?" -
"Yeah --
(Young Girl: Nothing there) -
c'mon we'll come up you better come with us -
we'll show you what that thing is" –

"Oh good" I said so I grabbed my spear iron spear -
tommyhawk in belt -
put my tommyhawk in my belt (Young Girl: Nothing
　　　there) -
naul karli karli –
an' iron spear we off –
to show me this place, huh! -

I was gonta laugh but I might frighten this thing
　　　(Laugh) -
I see these three old woman you know (Laugh) -
I see their track -
where they fall down everyside you know they get
　　　scratch blood everywhere in their arm -
all right -
we go -
(Whisper) "Jus' 'round this corner" they tell me "he's
　　　layin' down right in that, road" -
"Ah good" so we jus' turn around like this you know
　　　(Young Girl: Nothing there) I go slowly I leave
　　　these old people comin' behind all the womans
　　　me in front with the spear -
I look, I can see the road right through nothing --
I sing out (Whisper) "Where? where?" -
"In that fork road you know" they tell me (Laugh) -
"He's layin' down right there" he say "In dis way" -
"Yeah? but I can see all the road -
two road see one turn this way nother one there and
　　　what in the middle nothing" I tell-em -
(Whisper) "Oh must be gone" -
"Oh well we go an' have a look might be dog might be
　　　donkey" -
so we went right up there an' have a look oh all wet
　　　ground --
can't miss seeing the track -
"Where youfella seen im?" -
"Here he's layin' down" -
"Where's the track" I tell-im -

nothing no track nothing -
ah that made me think back now that other thing this
      other two bloke seen -
"Ahh this is only, mus' be devil" I tell-im -
"Something live in this country you know" I tell-im –
"Aah all right" they say this never worry them no
      more -
so we come back couldn't find his track - (Rasping
      starts)
oh we laugh all the way (Laugh)
where these three woman bin falling down (Laugh) –
pick up all those billycan an' bag an' everything --
(Rasping stops) after that one you think we can get
      them three woman to go back again NO NOOO!
      (Laughs) (Tap tap) -
they won't go back (Rasping starts) –
they never go back again -------
(Rasping stops) that's about all

lardi

A *maban* and two young men are living in an outcamp. The young men try to shoot brolga as they come to drink at the trough. The *maban* tells them not to. The *maban* leaves and the young men lie in wait for a brolga. A brolga comes and they shoot it and take it back to camp. They cook and eat the brolga.

The *maban* comes back and tells them that they will get sick. The men get sick and the *maban* cures them.

The *maban* reveals that he had changed himself into the brolga.

LARDI

Yeah --
I can tell story, that whatname (Rasping) you know ----
that two --
man? ---
you know that ---
Lardi Lardi ----
that man ---
they used to camp in Anna Plains, station you know --
he had two, mate belongta him too -
in the outcamp[1] -------
and these two boy used to go alla time days 'n' days you
     know -
eeevery day they trouble these, brolga -
brolga ----
the bird want to come for drink (Stops rasping) --
but (Laughs) they humbug all the time you know[2] --
they go there (Tap tap) -
they had shotgun too --
you know from boss --
boss used to give them shotgun to kill bullock er, oh
     anything kangaroo[3] --
(Tap tap, rasping) ---

so this old fella ---
see he said to these two young fellas -
oh good friend old, friend (Laugh) ---
he used to tell them "Don't humbug these birds let-em
     come for drink" -
you know (Rasping stops, tap tap) ---

they couldn't get chance to come in for drink (Rasping
     starts) ----

so one day --- (Rasping stops)
this old man he went --
he went bush -
'nother place (Tap tap) not very far --
jus' walkin' round -
an' he left these two blokes, behind they waiting for ---
for this brolga --
they made shade this time in the trough ---

all right ---
this old fella went bush --
all right an' when they look hello they see one brolga
     coming -
one, ooh straight·up -
jus' lookin' round you know what kine Brolga he's
     looking this way that way he's coming straight for
     well[4] -
straight for the trough -
an' when they come close to the trough he jus' stand up
     straight -
right alongside -
an' this two bloke gettin' ready with the gun -
with the shotgun you know --
BANG got 'im knock 'im down --
'nother bloke run pick-im up --
pick-im up take-im back home (Rasping starts) ----
they know --
they can tell if he's fat or skinny --
you know they open his -- (Rasping stops)
wing you know like this they feel ooh they can see that
     big lump here you know his fat -
(Clap) oooh proper fat --

all right they say --
well we only got one they say -

"Before that oldman come you better clean-im up an'
    we'll cook-im an' have a feed" (Laughs) -
this two bloke -
before that oldman come -
this nearly, oh long way yet time for 'im he won't be
    back yet -
"So we'll have to clean" they clean im up make fire
    everything make hole for im everything finish -
all right when they, when they finish -
when they finish --
then they --
to pull-im out from fire -
tupella start to eat-im now -
ooh big feed, fat -
ooh very fat -
they eat-im (Rasping) aaaall up --
nothing left -
they eat the lot -
an' they couldn't leave-im because he's too fat -
they didn't want to leave-im for the oldfella too -
I dunno what made them --
to think --
because they can -- (Rasping stops)
one brolga is not enough for, lotta people you know -
they want to get a good feed two man -
so they did ------
yeah --

so that oldfella come back ---
mmm "Did you fella get any, anything?" -
"Yeah we got one" --
"Where that thing now?" -
"Oh finish, we bin finish-im" --
"Ohhh mus' be fat eh?" -
"Yes yes oh yes" they tell-im -
"We thought you not goin' to come back you know --
we thought you gone to station Anna Plain --
come little bit late eh?" -

"Yes" -
"Ahh" -
"Ah well tha's right then" he say (Laugh) -

so when they finish --
(Rasping starts) --
"All right" he said -
"Mm, he fat eh?" -
"Yeah" -
"Ahh --
I think you tupella might get sick soon" (Rasping stops)
    say -
"He be too fat you know -
might be you tupella get sick soon" --
"Yeah?" -
"Yeah" -
"Ah --
oh well, too late now we bin eat-im" (Laughs) -
'nother fella off now straight away --
they start to spew you know --
eeeegh eeeegh 'nother fella --
'nother one gone again straight up *beeeegheeegh* one
    fella there *eeegheeeeeeeegh* shit come out he go
    bbbbbbbbbbb (Laughter) -
eeeeeeaaagh bbbbbbbbb everything come out one time
    same time everything come out, you know -
two of them -
same --
oooh they bin, musta spew about five times 'till nothing
    left inside that thing I s'pose they mighta spew
    everything out -
but that fat too, made-im come this end (Laughs) --
so 'nother fella start again this side you know *beeeeeegh*
    bbbbbbbbb (Laughter) -
'nother one again *eeeeeagh bbbbbbbb* -
ahh finish he say "Oh, that old fella coming -
oh you better see us" -
he's *maban* too that man oh proper *maban* -

"You better see us" -
"All right" he tell-im "We got a whatname here --
you better --
have a look at us must be something wrong" -
"Yeah --
yeah" he say -
come up he rubbed these two fella you know[5] --
oh finish they stop now no more -
nobody spew now finish -
stop -
oh everything stop-im everything one time -
maban man that fella too -
Lardi Lardi --

"All right" he tell-im "well --
yeah --
you tupella right now?" he ask-em -
"Yeah we all right --
yeah" -
"You know what you pella bin eating?" -
"No ----
oh yes" they say "Yeah we bin eat that, bird -
yeah -
yeah" -
"You tupella reckon that's that bird you pella bin
        eating?" -
"Yeah" -
"Well that's me" he tell-im (Laughs) -
you know -
"You tupella bin humbuggin' round all the time in that
        trough --
these birds never come for drink you know, hunt-im out
        all time -
yeah --
I only bin jus' play-play with you tupella you know" he
        say -
and tha's -
"We bin eat YOU?" they bin tell-im -

"YEAH, I bin turn meself into whatname –
ah brolga *gurdurwayin*" you know we say gurdurwayin –
"that's me" -
"Ahhh" Oh they know-im too oh everybody know him -
this oldfella he's a proper *maban* too –
dis man –
so that's the finish --
you know –
Lardi Lardi --
(Rasping)

living ghost

Story One
A man with a family used to look after a trough at an outcamp. Every Friday he would ride a bicycle into the station to get provisions.

One day he got to Galway Well where he stopped for water, leaning his bicycle against the rail. Some stockmen who came along afterwards found bicycle tracks going everywhere.

They questioned the man later at the station, who denied knowledge of this. He said that it must have been a ghost. On his way back he had a look at the well again. There were no tracks.

Story Two
Paddy as a little boy camped in the same place, with other people. In the middle of the night they heard a baby crying, so they lit fires in all the camps. After that they heard the sound of the crying die away.

Story Three
Later when Paddy was grown up he camped there while mustering sheep for La Grange. He let the horses and donkey go at night with bells so he could find them in the morning. In the morning he got up and followed the sound of the bells. But the sound took him further and further away in what turned out to be the wrong direction. When the sun was up, he suddenly heard the sound of the bells in the direction of the camp where somebody had already got the horses. There had been a murder in the vicinity.

LIVING GHOST

Story One

Well this fella used to look after the trough he had -
oh he had childrens too -
he had childrens -
he had about five or six children --
and a old lady -
mother for the children -
old man -

so this old man had a bicycle –
you know he gotta go back to station to get his tucker -
every friday -
he must go and get his tucker –
he carried, ration in the bicycle (Laugh) -
hard work --

so one day on friday that old fella start now -
from his place he went to Galway --
"Oh must get a drink of water" he said you know he
        went to Galway –
when he went to Galway get water he left his bicycle
        there --
on the rail you know --
left it on the rail just layin' against the rail -
he went there and -
chucked the bucket down get some water for himself
        that's the windlass too, you know –
oh this is not long -

67

not very long -
this is true story you know -
so -
all right -
when he drink his water he --
he come out when he finish grab his bicycle and off he
        go -
straight for station --
when he went to station -
oh that was, friday that's right -
and somebody come behind him -
all the stockboys you know -
with the horses -
no bullock but they'd come back from branding -
they come back now -

(High) they pull-up there -
"Hello" he say -
they see one bicycle track --
"Oh that oldfella musta go for his tucker --
get his ration from station" -
"Yeah yeah" --
so they come right up to the well -
in that well they see his track, oh Chris' bicycle track
        everywhere --
all over the place (Laugh) -
what the hell this old bloke was doin' (Laughs) you
        know --
oh track everywhere --
bicycle track -
when he took off only one man -
but round the well, oh bicycle track everywhere -
running round -
only one man -

all right when they, when they go to station -
"Hey" say "what wrong with you you bin get mad?" -
"What for?" -

"What you bin doin' in Galway?" -
"Ah I only bin drink water" he say --
"Yeah but what --
your track everywhere -
with bicycle running around" -
"No no no no" he say "not me" -
"Yes" -
"No I left my bicycle in the rail I went inside -
pull the water up and drink and off I went" -
"Ahh no no no track everywhere" --
so ---
"Ah" --
ah, well he know -
yeah -
"Might be too" he say -
"But not me -
I know what happened ---
I know what happened" --
he got living ghost there too -
in that well -
you know he's in the scrub -
woman -
he's a woman he got baby ---
"Might be that one" he say -
you know he tell these fellas --
"Oh, oh well that's right" they tell 'im --
(High) when he went back again past that well he pull
        up there again --
he look ah no (Laugh) no track nothing -
only same track he come from this side you know -
and he left his bicycle there -
no track oh this lot must be liar they must be gettin'
        silly ---
so he went back straight back to his camp ----

well that's true too -
he got living ghost there you know aalways -
woman that boy little baby

69

Story Two

So one day I camped there too with my people, you
     know when I was a little boy --
I camped there with my people -
old people you know mother and father --
couple more others too --
we camped there we made a fire --
but fire went down -
you know slow down like this one -
but 'nuf fire for us you know -
he slow down -
so we all went to sleep --
in that same well -
but 'way from the road you know -
all right -
first thing we hear little baby cry -
little baby -
cry -
crying -
(Breathy) "Oh baby baby crying -
yeah yeah" oh 'nother fella come -
"Oh yes yeah yeah that's right" he tell 'em -
"We better light the fire" -
so they light the fire in every camp you know make a
     biiig fire --
and you can hear this fella too when the baby was
     crying you can hear 'im (Slap slap slap) (Laugh) -
Oh I heard this one too -
that one -
so we made a big fire you can hear the baby crying
     looong way now he's gone --
you can't hear the mother -
only baby crying ----
he's a living ghost you know ---
well they only just say *wirang* --
wirang you know he belonga there --
(Soft) *wirang* he belonga there

Story Three

That's one now -
this time I was big man -
already I was a man -
and we went through there too with ah, sheep -
oh we was coming back anyway from La Grange with
        the sheep -
an' we camp in that Galway -
but not there up in the hill -
(Soft) little bit more higher up you know -
we camp there --

all right -
I didn't know too ---
so we jus' camp -
oh I know from small time but I never think about no
        more anything you know --
soo --
we sleep all night we made a yard you know for sheep -
bushes yard -
put all the sheep in the yard and we lie down go to
        sleep -
I watch these horses now -
it's all plain country -
oh little hills here and there -
er like this here you know close to the sea -
he very close to sea too –

so, all right ---
"Oh I better, have it here where the bell?" I said you
        know I'm a horse trailer too I gotta get up early in
        the morning get horses -
all right -
I hear these horses "Oh that's right, the bell is gone that
        way" -
It's true too because lotta feed up this side you know -
donkey horse two bells aall feeding there you know -

good grass you know -
green grass -

all right -
we went to sleep -
in the morning I get up -
in the morning I get up -
oh, 'bout three o'clock in the morning I think -
I get up -
(Breathy) I listen wind -
for the bell -
I know where the bell this way you know --
this way two bell donkey and horse -
bell you know -
ah go back to sleep again oh just have a laydown you
     know --
mm I put my ears out again -
I hear oh yes this way -
so I grabbed my bridle, off -
that's about four o'clock in the mornin' -
I went -
I followed that bell -
aall the way -
walkin' round -
I got my bridle -
I stop again I -
put my ears out -
oh yes two bells -
that's right (Laugh) -
still loong way yet --
it was all plain country you know I start running --
in the good -
good ground where 's no grass -
I want to get the horses quick -
so we can let the sheep out -
early you know -
I listen again -
oh not far -

not far now -
so sun already gettin' bright now -
keep going keep going keep going keep going keep
     going -
(Soft) I listen again -
I put my ears again -
oh sun already now he's all bright now -
aall bright -
I listen —
this way "Ding ding" (Laugh) -
(Breathy) behind -
but the other bloke got the horses dis side -
and donkey -
they already in the camp -
an' I'm over here (Laugh) -
yeah this the thing made me mad -
you know "Oh" -
I come back running -
oh sun already sun up now -
jus' sun peeping out you know -
"Where you bin?" -
tell me -
"Ohohoo --
something wrong" I said --
I tell 'em all this bell you know I heard the bell this
     way -
"Yeah yeah that's right" -
well this old fella tell me -
well dis hill where we camping now –
that's where -
we bin bury one oldman before -
one tree there you know -
long time somebody musta kill him -
somebody musta kill him because he's a stranger -
he come from dis side oh somewhere from ---
oh not Roy Hill but more this side you know --
these people -
these pearlers used to take them on the lugger –

73

an' he didn't like this country he wanted to go back on
    foot -
but they got 'im there they kill 'im -
he's a strange man you know -
(Soft) they didn't know who he --

so that's the thing made me wrong - (Laugh)
that made me -
we camp right there where the old man -
they bury the old fella there too -
oh not old fella he's only young man too -
you know middle-aged -
lotta things wrong

djaringgalong

Djaringgalong, a monster bird, used to steal babies and take them home to eat. Two men went to have a look at his nest and found two eggs. They went back to get two *maban*.

The two maban went to the bird's nest and waited all night for it. In the morning they attacked and speared it. The bird turned into stars.

DJARINGGALONG

That's *Djaringgalong*[1] -
(Stephen: Yeah) he used to travel from there ---
Djaringgalong you know he used to travel from there ---
he come up here to pick up lil'-lil' fellas -
you know that's for his -
nest to feed his -
young ones -
he gotta get something for them to eat -
but he pick up -
babies from there –
boy girl anyone babies -
when he pick these fellas up then he go back all time
    back here to his nes' -
feed all his -
young ones too –
well, that time he didn' have any young ones yet,
    really --
that fella didn' have any young ones yet he only had
    two eggs --
you know, he musta eat these himself too[2] –
every afternoon he go out -
pick-em-up he come back again towards morning ---

so -----
so one day come these people -
belong to this part of the country -
I dunno who they are but this part of the country they
    find out --
you know big bird always pick up -

whatname -
oh these two man went firs' they had a look under that
      tree --
but nobody was on top -
they look "Oh" two eggs --
an' bone head everything all kids -
you know, bone -
"Oh this fella eating -
this fella eating people -
this bird --"
so distupella climb up an' have a look --
you know "Ah two egg" -
they see two egg on top -
"Oh" baby one baby half eatened up you know only
      bone -
in the whatname, in that nest -
but he's bin eatin' that one you know he himself the
      mother one --
all right they said er "I think we'll have to get this
      one" -
you know -
this is all bone --
these two man they wen' back an' they tell these
      fellas ---
"Any good *maban* we got here?" --
you knooow to kill this -
Djaringgalong -
they know *Djaringgalong* too -
"Yes" they tell-im -
"We got two man" --
oh plenty man was there but they get the bes' one -
two bes' man --
if he, there's lot more man there if they oughta go they
      get kill you know but they get the two bes' man -
they bring-im-up -
these two man dress up with they -
they dress up -
they get their two spears -

78

an' that whatname -
we call-im (Question to Donald in Nyingina) *garbarda*
    eh? (Donald: Mm)[3] -
gurdjarda we call-im he got that -
woomera too -
wooden spear right through[4] -
one each -
an' --
well we call-im this one ---
garbina you know but we call-im *nyigabai* -
yarda yarda[5] -
we call-im -
he dance with that one and he got his thing hooked on
    (Laugh)[6] –

tupella hide away ---
tupella hide away in the --
oooh big woolly tree you know underneath so this fella
    can' see them -
they look, only egg -
oh tupella go back to their place -
they wait for-im you know what time he gonna
    comeback -
wait wait wait wait wait aaaall night -
(Soft) all night -
just about towards morning -
just about towards morning -
tjipeee they hear-im -
he's coming they can hear-im -
somewhere here - (Laugh)
they hear-im he's comin' back -
so they get ready these two bloke -
(Soft) these two bloke get ready -
(Soft) all right tupella start firs' -
he's a *maban* too that bird -
big *maban* ---

when they come down -

right he come riiight up this fella -
he fly fly fly fly he land right in his, nest -
when this, bird land in his nest -
ooooh shake the country - (Bang with hand on ground)
you know when he land (Laugh) -
biig heavy thing -
(Soft) when he land —

all right he look round everywhere -
it's just about gettin' -
sunrise you know sun gettin' up ooh well gettin' bright -
they never come out in the dark -
they wait 'til the sun gettup -
then he look -
"Aah" he can smell something too -
this fella on top but he's lookin' round where? -
(Laugh, speaks to Donald) *binabinaba* -
he smelling you know everywhere -
now he's lookin' 'round must be somebody here -
he's on the watch now he never eat these boys what he
        bring you know two -
he's watching -
(Soft) watching -
when the sun gettup "Ah go on" -
'nother man said to his 'nother man "All right you first -
you first" -
so this man gettup -
you know he dance -
he dance with his whatname? -
with that *yarda* an' that thing? -
he dance -
straight for his nest you know come up this way -
oh long way -
he want this fella to come down to grab im -
that thing seen im "Oh man haha" he gettin ready now
        this fella -
(Sustains high pitch) he come down from the tree want
        to grab that bloke no missed-im (Laugh) -

that man too clever for im -
he come out other side -
come back again -
that eaglehawk turn round again come back again he
　　　want to grab im again nooo that fella was right
　　　level with the ground -
he couldn' get im (Laugh) ─
from there then 'nother fella come up -
'nother one come out -
that's two of them now -
while he was playin' around he want to grab this man
　　　'nother one come out -
went down an' he jus' want to climb up this fella throw
　　　spear for im right through (Laugh) -
finish knocked im down -
then other fella come up -
'nother spear again finish -
they finish im off -
they killed im -
finish -
no more *Djaringgalong* -
that time -

well if they didn' kill this *Djaringgalong* -
today the *Djaringgalong* oughta be still living -
but they kill that one -
an' they break the two eggs too -
finish no more baby born -
that's his first egg -
finish ─
if they didn' kill im *Djaringgalong* oughta been in this
　　　country -
(Stephen: But he's in other world now) -
he's in other world -
he's finish now -
finish -
there was only one *Djaringgalong* -
well ─

he's not a really –
he's not a really bird he's er, something big thing you
     know --
one -
from that egg now must be lotta things *Djaringgalong*
     oughta breed them you know --
but lucky they got im before they breed -
that's why no *Djaringgalong* this time (Stephen: Ah) -
that's the finish

langgur

Langgur, the possum, used to be a man. He didn't like having too many people living around him so he decided to get rid of them. He came to a camp of people one day and led them back to his place, ostensibly for a corroborree. When they got there, Langgur had disappeared into the hollow tree where he lived. After a while the people began to get thirsty, so they called out to Langgur asking him for water. He refused, so all the people died.

Next time he wanted to do the same thing with another group. But two *maban* men had dreamt about his activities. So when he arrived they humoured him right up to when he refused water. When he refused the two maban men pulled him down from the tree by his legs and chopped his head off. Then they chopped off a knot on the tree trunk and the water flowed out in great quantities reviving the dead people.

LANGGUR

Yeah-
yeah well this -
all right? -
this *langgur[1]* -
possum -
but he used to be true, true person you know before -
man walking around --

so one day he --
he was thinkin' about --
there's too many people -
you know walkin' round everywhere --
an he didn' like er -
he like to be on his own -
all the time you know he don't like too many people
      walkin' round everywhere --
they kill too much -
killing too much animal I s'pose you know lizards and
      things -
that's why he didn' want these fellas so one day he
      think about I think I know how to get rid of these
      fellas -

so he went to one place where big mob of people -
camping -
one waterhole they look hello they say -
they look "Ooh heere grandfather coming" -
but they call 'im *djambardu* -
"Here *djambardu* coming" -

85

grandfather you know in English -
"*Djambardu* coming" –
HE HE he laugh you know when he come HEM -
"Yes *djambardu* what you bin come for" -
"I bin come for you fellas -
somebody bin send me from there we got biig
     kabbakabba on^2 -
(Laugh) so aall you fellas we gotta bring the lot -
I gotta bring aaall you fellas gotta follow me -
biig *kabbakabba* will be on"-
"Oh good -
when we can leave?" -
"Tomorrow straight away" -
"All right (Laugh) -
all right -
aah -
now -
some crippled man -
some blind man" -
he had two in this mob -
"All right -
now -
tomorrow -
what about these crippled people? -
and these blind man?" -
"Oooh we must bring them too they gotta hear this -
they gotta see this *kabbakabba* you know" he say -
"We gotta bring" -
"Yeah but how we gonta carry these crippled man?" -
"Oh we'll carry 'em, plenty people here we'll carry 'em
     change about you know (Laugh) -
blind man, we'll lead 'em along too" -
might be two or three blind man you know -
well they take everything all this people -
he bring the lot riight up to his place -
where that -
tree is -
you know his tree -

"All right" he say -
they camp halfway -
one night -
next day they get right up to that tree that's his
        camping ground -
this possum you know -
Langgur -
when he come up there -
(Soft) when he come up there -
"All right this is the place" he tell 'em -
"We gotta stop -
we gotta wait for this lot now -
stop quiet -
don't let these, children run around everywhere you
        know -
tell-em to stop quiet -
somebody will be here soon with -
corroboree you know they come out from somewhere -
aah –"
all right "Well you fella will be all right here" -
you know they all sit around this tree an' here's the
        tree -
an' he off from here now he was preaching these people
        he off he go there he climb up the tr' -
"Where you goin' *djambardu?*" -
"Ah I only have a look here -
I climb up this tree" (Laugh) mm so when he climbed
        up this tree -
branch he get in from there he got his hole you know
        big -
holler tree -
he go inside right in –
but he was –
but he was only liar you know heeee want to go back
        there -
he got inside and they can hear this -
fella you know he's -
he's drinkin' water -

inside -

ah -
all right after while all the lil'-lil' fellas cry now they
    want water you know -
an' big people -
all right -
(Calls out) "*Djambardu* you give us water" -
(Breathy) he come out -
he peep -
from you know (Laugh) hollow tree he peep from
    hollow tree -
shhhh (Laugh) --
put 'em all down you know -
tell 'em to (Breathy) "Stop stop" -
"Somebody will be here soon" -
(Soft) ah -
all go down now -
he went inside again have his -
oh just have a laydown inside -
aall night -
you know -

so some people ooh in coupla days -
finish -
lil'-lil' fellas aall dead now (Laugh) -
well the big people too -
now all this mob all dead finish -
he climb up again he have a look -
"*Djambardu* you give us water -
all the people dead now" -
"Yeaah" he say -
"Who bin tell you fella to come up here?" -
"Well you tell us he got c'roborree here" -
"No I never bring you fellas here" (Laugh) -
oh he get cheeky the oldfella you know -
"Ah" -
"He all right" -

"All right all right all right" he say -
"I go an' get water now" -
he go down again -
next day he come out he look -
oh still coupla blokes kicking -
'nother lot all finish (Laugh) -
you know jus' moving around lil' bit -
go back again -
next day he get up aall dead finish -
then he come out -

all right aall these people dead now finish -
aall these people all dead -
so next day he off again -
to 'nother water hole -
next day he off to 'nother water hole -
go right up -
to pick these fellas up -
he come out in oooh few people -
but he had two *maban* there[3] -
two *maban* man -
ooh this two *maban* man say ooh that *Langgur* -
he say -
Langgur the man his name *Langgur* -
that fella now, possum -
hee he always pick-im-up people he take - 'em there an'
      he want to kill-'em -
you know -
he no good bad man -
"Yeah" -
"Yeah" -
he had two *maban* -
but we'll wait anyway might be nothing -
oh, they wait in that camp might be nothing -
you know -
might be nothing -
they look "Oh" -
here he come out true -

"Oho (Laugh) oh *djambardu*" -
djambardu djambardu djambardu djambardu they say
  djambardu grandfather you know *djambardu* aaall
  us mob -
"Oh ha ha" he laugh mm -
"What you bin come for?" -
"Oh we got *kabbakabba* somebody bin send me,
  youpella must come aaall you fellas again" he
  tell-im -
"We gotta go tomorra" -
ooh they camp that night -
next mornin' -
they take -
oh might be coupla blind man too you know -
they bring-im all -
"But we'll leave some of these people here I think old
  old fellas" -
noo no no no we gotta take-im whole lot -
whole lot whole lot -
sloowly we go they go sloowly you know right up -
he bring 'im back again he come back this time hee
  make his camp here -
(Laugh) you know -
here - (Draws)
this side -
they didn' see these fellas (Laugh) -
they're other side -
oh good way from tree like you know from here to -
(Soft) mm sea -
all right this lot say (Sniff) mm (Sniff sniff) -
(Breathy) "*Djambardu* -
they say what that one smell -
might be somebody bin -
somebody? -
something bin dead somewhere?"
"Shhhh" (Breathy) he say -
"Shhhh this one no good -
don't youpella talk" say -

90

"No good" -

this is the c'roborree" he say "*Kabbakabba* now I bin
    bring you fella for" -

"Ooh" -

"Stop quiet" -

but these two *maban* know he tell all these fellas too -

they watch-im -

(Soft) this old man he come up here's the tree belonga
    him he go there -

he was preaching here you know -

he come back again he climb up his tree again same hole
    he go in -

(Soft) he go in -

all right now these two *maban* man say -

these two *maban* man say -

now you fella get ready -

(Soft) all right straight away they ask-im -

you know they can hear-im inside you know clean his
    water out - *glok glok glok glok* inside the holler
    tree you know (Laugh) everywhere -

(Calls out) "All right *djambardu*" he say -

"You give us drink water", nobody dead yet -

"You give us drink water" -

"Oh no got water he say" -

"No water" -

"Yeah but -

all the little fellas all crying they want drink water" -

"Oh never mind" he say -

"What for you fella bin come up leave you fella water"
    (Laugh) -

"Well you bin bring us up here" -

"Noo not me" say (laugh) he climb up his tree -

so these two *maban* man they get their tommyhawks,
    stone tommyhawk must be -

no you know stone tommyhawk -

we know -

he got that -

you know that hollow, some trees they got this lump -

lump (Stephen: Yeah) lump -
they come up they cut that tree -
dud dud -
that lump come out you know water run everywhere -
finish -
run everywhere -
"Hoh" he look "Oh" -
he climb up the tree they grab-im from (Laugh) -
leg this two man grab-im -
grab the *langgur* -
he was man -
finish they cut his head off with the axe (Laugh) -
with that stone tommyhawk kill-im finish -
kill that man -
water was running everywhere -
so when that water run everywhere -
an' these dead people -
now they aall come up life again -
they move about now (Laugh) -
finish -
I dunno how but he's *bugaregara* anyway -
they all come live again (Stephen: Mm) -
that's that *Langgur* now, possum

Notes

Mirdinan

1. *Karnun* is the local Aboriginal name for Fisherman's Bend.
2. This could be translated as "his wife knew a Malay man who was on a boat in the creek". The story refers to events which probably occurred in the early 1920's when many Malays, Japanese and Chinese were working in the booming pearling industry.
3. The pearling luggers were flat-bottomed and would be left dry in the creeks at low tide.
4. "Coming back with nothing" is a motif in these stories which indicates that something has gone wrong.
5. *yunmi* means "you and me".
6. Mirdinan points to something to avert her gaze.
7. "belongs to" means they were in a certain relationship, brother and sister in this case.
8. Many Aboriginal prisoners were brought into town in this way.
9. A *maban* is an Aboriginal "doctor". These are men or women who are well-trained in Aboriginal law and have special perceptive skills or fighting skills.
10. A "growling" voice used in disbelief, or to admonish someone, disperse dogs, etc.
11. A "true story" is like a legend. It is about identifiable people and events in the not-too-distant past. This classification is opposed to *bugaregara* stories (stories of the "dreaming"). The interruption also occurs at a structural break in the story.
12. "Flatform" is a linguistic hypercorrection. Since Aboriginal languages lack "f" sounds, these are mostly pronounced like "p". Somebody over-correcting their "p's" will therefore produce words such as this.

13. Butcher Joe Nangan.
14. *Waragan* is the word for eaglehawk in Nyigina.
15. *Djabi* is a type of "popular" Aboriginal song, found also throughout the Pilbara. See: C.G. von Brandenstein and A.P. Thomas, *Tarura – Aboriginal Song Poetry from the Pilbara*, Adelaide, Rigby, 1974.
16. *mabu* (Nyigina) means "good", "finished". This song was sung in unison by Paddy Roe and Butcher Joe Nangan. The words in bold lettering indicates their singing together, while the single underlining indicates Butcher Joe alone.
17. The judge.
18. The "belly" is seen as the location of personal power and personal feelings.
19. The listener is being tested to see if he remembers the name.
20. He is meaning Butcher Joe.
21. A certain amount of text, concerning the kinship of Mirdinan to Broome people was edited at this point.
22. "gibim" is "give him".
23. The narrator is pointing out that this is a public rather than a secret story.

Duegara

1. *buga wamba* means "bad man" and refers to a phallus-shaped stone at Fisherman's bend.
2. One of the five seasons, as indicated in the Nyigina language.
3. This place is charted in the "dreaming" stories.

Worawora Woman

1. A "proper" man is of flesh and blood, as opposed to spirits.
2. After going through the appropriate procedure of painting oneself with green paint made from the leaves of a certain tree, a man who goes out and waits might meet up with the spirit woman called *worawora*. He can have sexual relations with her, but both she and her tracks will remain invisible to all but the man who has painted himself.
3. She is collecting the food in her coolamon, a wooden dish.
4. At an appropriate break in the story, Butcher Joe tries to find out if the smoke is making me uncomfortable.

Yaam

1. This story was told by Paddy Roe as he was rasping a boomerang. The noises have been noted because they tend to punctuate the story.
2. A Catholic Brother from Beagle Bay Mission.
3. "Cranky" means mad.
4. *naul(u)* = hitting stick
   karli = boomerang
5. Yaam feels he should be punished on entering the camp because he is the last of his tribe, and had "lost" his people.
6. They were making fun of him.
7. *rai* are invisible spirits who can be seen only by *maban*, appear in dreams, and can occasionally be glimpsed by ordinary people.

Donkey Devil

1. At this time (World War II) the Japanese were bombing Broome.
2. An interjection from Paddy Roe's great-grand-daughter, who predicts what he is going to say.

Lardi

1. These men had the job of keeping a windmill and trough in order.
2. "humbug" means "cause a nuisance".
3. A lot of trouble was caused by the mis-match of economic systems in the early days of European colonization of the area. Aborigines who were used to hunting anything on their land didn't understand, initially at least, the whites accumulation of animals for sale at distant markets. Spearing of cattle by Aborigines led to disputes between them and settlers and sometimes to punitive expeditions (massacres) of Aborigines by police patrols.
4. "kine" means "kind"; the way the brolga walks.
5. Massage as trauma therapy.

Djaringgalong

1. Compare the story of *Djaringgalong* in Nangan and Edwards, 1976.
2. A slight error was made in the narration, which was corrected by this statement.
3. Donald is a countryman of Paddy Roe.
4. A spear which is a solid piece of wood, rather than the Northern Kimberley variety which has a bamboo shaft.
5. *yarda* is a shield.
6. Dancing with the spear hooked onto his spear-thrower.

Langgur

1. Compare the story of "Midjina The Wicked Wizard and the Garadjeri" in Nangan and Edwards, 1976.
2. *kabbakabba* means "corroboree".
3. This means: *There were two maban there.*

Paddy Roe

Well in Roebuck Plains Station, I s'pose -
sheep station, eh? -
(Stephen: Yeah) -
old sheep station -
well where I born -
I born in sheep station -
old sheep station used to be old sheep station -
but it's finished now, but the springs is still there -
but them springs, they're my *tjila* -
my spirit -
you know -
then I come out then (Laugh) –
baby, you know -
(Krim Benterrak: Mm) -
but that's my spirit -
an' I been, running around

Paddy Roe was born just before the First World War in
about 1912. He grew up on Roebuck Plains Station,
near Broome in the north-west of Western Australia. He
worked for many years as a drover and a windmill
repairer throughout the Kimberley region. He is
patriarch of a large family and has been a widower for
many years.

He has a good deal of knowledge of his traditional
society and maintains a position of power as a kind of
ombudsman negotiating between governmental agencies
and the Aboriginal communities of the Broome region.

Stephen Muecke

Stephen Muecke was born in Adelaide, South Australia, in 1951, but was brought up and educated in Newcastle and Melbourne. After receiving a degree in French and Linguistics at Monash University, he taught for a year at the University of Western Australia. Then, as a research officer in the Department of Anthropology, he worked in the Kimberley for the first time, in 1975.

He spent the next year doing a master's degree in Linguistics in Paris and became interested in French theories of narrative. When he came back to the University of Western Australia to do a doctorate, he applied these theories in the analysis of contemporary Aboriginal narratives in the Kimberley.

This book is the first major publication to come out of this research. Other papers of a more theoretical nature have appeared in academic journals. Stephen Muecke has produced a further book with Paddy Roe (and Krim Benterrak), *Reading The Country*. He is also co-editor of an anthology of Aboriginal writing, *Paperbark*.

Stephen Muecke now lives in Sydney and is Associate Professor in the School of Humanities at the University of Technology, Sydney, in the area of Communication Studies.